Don't Eat the Babysitter!

ISBN-13: 978-0-545-01531-8
ISBN-10: 0-545-01531-6

Copyright © 2004 by Nick Ward. All rights reserved.
Published by Scholastic Inc., 557 Broadway, New York, NY 10012,
by arrangement with Random House Children's Books, a division of Random House, Inc.
SCHOLASTIC and associated logos are trademarks and/or registered trademarks of Scholastic Inc.

12 11 10 9 8 7 6 5 4 3 2 1   8 9 10 11 12/0

Printed in the U.S.A.   40

First Scholastic printing, May 2007

Don't Eat the Babysitter!

Nick Ward

SCHOLASTIC INC.

New York   Toronto   London   Auckland   Sydney
Mexico City   New Delhi   Hong Kong   Buenos Aires

*For Eileen and Tony
and babysitters everywhere*

Sammy and Sophie Shark were very excited! Mom and Dad had gone out for the evening and Anna, their favorite babysitter, had come to look after them.

But when Sammy became too excited, he had the unfortunate habit (as all young sharks do) of biting things!

"Supper's ready," called Anna.
"What is it?" asked Sammy,
rushing into the room.
"It's your favorite," said Sophie.
"Kiddie Fingers!"

"Yummy!" cheered Sammy.

He opened his mouth and...

CRUNCH!

"Oh Sammy," cried Sophie.
"Don't eat the supper tray!"
"Sorry," said Sammy.
"Never mind," said Anna.
"Let's play a game of cards."

"Great," cried Sammy.
"Er...what do we do?"
"We turn the cards over," explained Anna,
"and if two cards match, the first one
to shout SNAP! wins."

They started to turn over their cards. First Anna, then Sophie, and then Sammy. His tail twitched with excitement.

"SNAP!" shouted Sophie when she saw two cards the same. "I won!"
"That's not fair," said Sammy.

"Never mind, Sammy,"
said Anna. "Let's play again."
Anna turned over another card.
Then Sammy went...

CRUNCH!

"Oh Sammy!" said Sophie. "It's SNAP, not CRUNCH!"
"Sorry," said Sammy, blushing. "I didn't mean to."

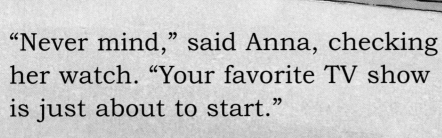

"Never mind," said Anna, checking her watch. "Your favorite TV show is just about to start."

Anna turned on the television.
"Terrors of the Deep!" said the announcer.

"Yeah!" shouted Sammy,
and they settled down to watch.
Sammy's tail twitched with excitement.

"Deep in the inky black ocean," said the television, "lives the awesome giant octopus. He's huge and he's fierce and yum, yum, yum, he eats little sharks for breakfast!"

"Oh, NO!"
shouted Sammy.
He opened his mouth and...

"Oh Sammy," gasped Sophie.
"Don't eat the television!"
"Sorry," gulped Sammy. "It was an accident."
"Never mind," smiled Anna.
"It's time for your bath now."

Sammy and Sophie loved bath time.
Sophie spread some bubbles on top
of a big yellow sponge.

"Who wants a piece of my
lovely sponge cake?" she asked.
"Me," cried Sammy, all in a lather.

He opened his mouth and...

CRUNCH!

"Oh Sammy," sighed Sophie.
"Don't eat the bath!"
"Sorry," spluttered Sammy.
"Never mind dear," said Anna.
"I think it's time for bed now."

"But I'm not tired," yawned Sammy
as Anna kissed him goodnight.
"I'm not tired," he mumbled as she
turned off the light.
"Just think of nice things," said Anna.
"You'll soon drift off to sleep."
"I'm not..." and Sammy fell fast asleep!

Supercod

W.W.F.
Whale Wrestling Federa

Sammy dreamt of his favorite things. He dreamt of a big squashy marshmallow, and...

CRUNCH!

went his pillow.

He dreamt of a big bar of chocolate, and...

CRUNCH!

went his dresser.

He dreamt of a big juicy burger, and...

went his bed.

"Wake up, Sammy," called Sophie. "You're eating the bedroom!"

"What's all this noise?"
asked Anna the babysitter,
diving into the room.
Sammy was dreaming
of a giant Kiddie Finger!

He opened his mouth and...

"SAMMY!" cried Sophie.

"DON'T
EAT THE..."

Just then, Mom and Dad arrived home, and Sammy woke up.

"Hello darlings," said Mom. "Have you been good?"

"Well!" giggled Sophie. "Sammy ate the TV and the supper tray, and the cards, and the bath, and the bedroom and..."

"Where's Anna?" asked Mom.
"Yes, where's Anna?" said Dad.
"Oh Sammy," they cried,

"you didn't eat the..."

"No, here I am!" laughed Anna, "and they've both been very good little sharks ...
Haven't you, Sammy?"

But for once, Sammy kept his mouth firmly

SHUT!

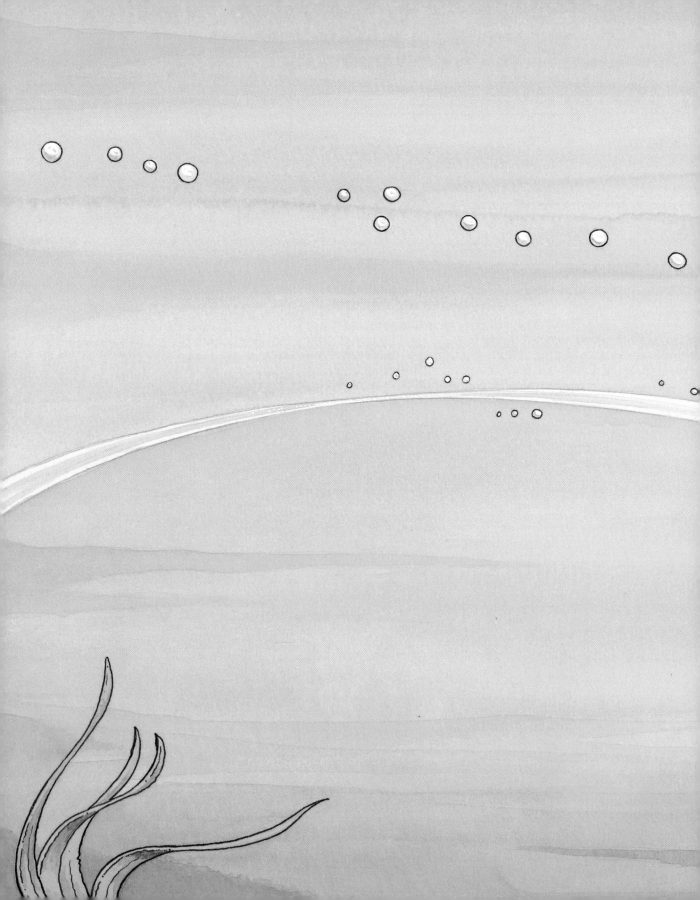